This book belongs to:

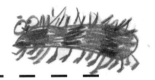

_ _

For Endaf.
With special thanks to Helen Mortimer, Sarah Darby
and Jason Taylor for their creative support.

Nicola and Charlotte

OXFORD
UNIVERSITY PRESS

Great Clarendon Street, Oxford OX2 6DP

Oxford University Press is a department of the University of Oxford.
It furthers the University's objective of excellence in research, scholarship,
and education by publishing worldwide in

Oxford   New York

Auckland Cape Town Dar es Salaam Hong Kong Karachi
Kuala Lumpur Madrid Melbourne Mexico City Nairobi
New Delhi Shanghai Taipei Toronto

With offices in

Argentina Austria Brazil Chile Czech Republic France Greece
Guatemala Hungary Italy Japan Poland Portugal Singapore
South Korea Switzerland Thailand Turkey Ukraine Vietnam

Oxford is a registered trade mark of Oxford University Press
in the UK and in certain other countries

British Library Cataloguing in Publication Data available

ISBN: 978-0-19-273232-3 (paperback)

2 4 6 8 10 9 7 5 3 1

Printed in China

Paper used in the production of this book is a natural,
recyclable product made from wood grown in sustainable forests.
The manufacturing process conforms to the environmental
regulations of the country of origin

CHARLOTTE MIDDLETON
presents

CHRISTOPHER'S
Caterpillars

a tale of minibeasts and mystery!

OXFORD
UNIVERSITY PRESS

If there was one thing
Christopher Nibble **loved** almost as much
as playing football, it was gardening.

Christopher's dandelions were the tastiest in the whole of Dandeville. They had even won prizes.

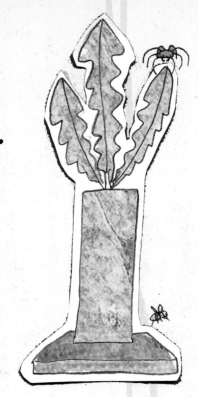

But growing prize-winning plants . . .

was too much work for one guinea pig.

So Christopher was very pleased
when he met a guinea pig called Posie.

Christopher and Posie worked
in the garden together.

They also played football and went on picnics. Soon they became the best of friends.

One day, Christopher heard a strange
sound coming from his dandelions.

munch

crunch

crunch

munch

crunch

crunch

SIX VERY HAIRY CATERPILLARS were eating his
prize plants. They looked awfully happy!

Christopher didn't know what to do. He couldn't possibly leave them munching his dandelions.

Then Posie had a marvellous idea to keep the caterpillars . . .

as pets! Christopher and Posie wrote a list
of all the things they might need
to look after their caterpillars.

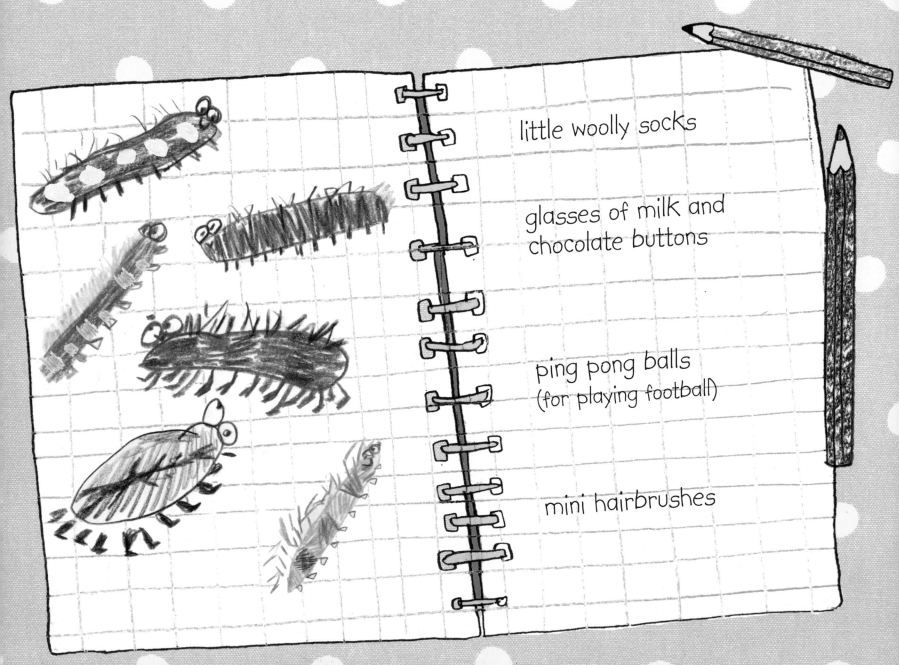

little woolly socks

glasses of milk and
chocolate buttons

ping pong balls
(for playing football)

mini hairbrushes

And they took it to Mr Rosetti in the café. He knew everything about everything.

Mr Rosetti looked at the list
and made a few suggestions.

✗ little woolly socks

✓ clean jars

✗ glasses of milk and
chocolate buttons

✓ juicy leaves for
munching

✗ ping pong balls
(for playing football)

✓ twigs for climbing

✗ mini hairbrushes

✓ lids with holes for
plenty of fresh air

He even had some clean jars to give to
Christopher and Posie. He told them how
to look after their new pets so that
they knew exactly what to do.

Christopher and Posie loved their new pets.

They were the happiest caterpillars in Dandeville.

they were gone!

Not a single wriggling caterpillar to be seen.
Not a single munching sound to be heard.

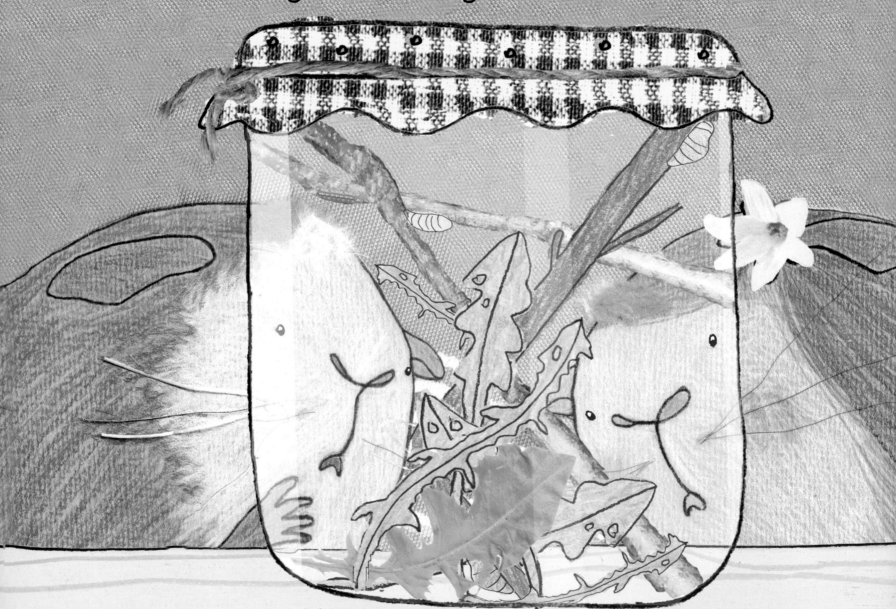

It was quite a mystery.

But Christopher and Posie were determined
to solve the mystery of their missing pets.
They made some posters . . .

and put them up
all over Dandeville.

Posie and Christopher were worried — nobody had seen their caterpillars.

Then an email from Mr Rosetti
popped up in Christopher's inbox.

From: Mr ROSETTI
To: CHRISTOPHER
Subject: Lost Caterpillars!

Please bring your sweet jars to the café.

Mr Rosetti examined the jars. Very carefully he lifted off the lids. And out of the jars flew . . .

six beautiful butterflies.

'You see,' said Mr Rosetti,
'when you lose a caterpillar,
you find a butterfly.'
The mystery was solved!

Christopher and Posie made some new posters . . .

so that the guinea pigs of Dandeville would know what had happened to the caterpillars.

And because the posters that Christopher and Posie had made were so eye-catching . . .

they were given pride of place
in Dandeville Art Gallery.